Imagination and the Letter I

Alphabet Friends

by Cynthia Klingel and Robert B. Noyed

The
**Child's
World**

The Child's World

Published in the United States of America
by The Child's World®
P.O. Box 326
Chanhassen, MN 55317-0326
800-599-READ
www.childsworld.com

The Child's World®: Mary Berendes, Publishing Director

Editorial Directions, Inc.: E. Russell Primm, Editorial
Director; Emily Dolbear, Line Editor; Ruth Martin,
Editorial Assistant; Linda S. Koutris, Photo Researcher
and Selector

Photographs ©: Myrleen Ferguson Cate/PhotoEdit:
Cover & 20; SW Productions/Photodisc/Getty Images:
10; Jeff Greenberg/PhotoEdit: 12; Corbis/Picture
Quest: 15; Stuart Westmorland/Stone/Getty Images:
16; Corbis: 19.

Library of Congress Cataloging-in-Publication Data
Klingel, Cynthia Fitterer.
   Imagination and the letter I / by Cynthia Klingel and
Robert B. Noyed.
      p. cm. — (Alphabet readers)
Summary: A simple story about the fun one can have
using one's imagination introduces the letter "i".
Includes bibliographical references (p.) and index.
   ISBN 1-59296-099-5 (alk. paper)
   [1. Imagination—Fiction. 2. Alphabet.] I. Noyed,
Robert B. II. Title. III. Series.
   PZ7.K6798Im 2003
   [E]—dc21   2003006535

Note to parents and educators:
The first skill children acquire before becoming successful readers is individual letter recognition. The Alphabet Friends series has been created with the needs of young learners in mind. Each engaging book begins by showing the difference between the capital letter and the lowercase letter. In each of the books on the vowels and the consonants c and g, children are introduced to the different sounds that the letter can make. Finally, children see that the letters can be found at the beginning of a word, in the middle of a word, and in most cases, at the end of a word.

Following the introduction, children meet their Alphabet Friends. The friend in each story encounters many words that include the featured letter of that book. Each noun that begins with the title letter is highlighted in red with the initial letter of the word in bold. Above the word is a rebus drawing that establishes a strong picture cue.

At the end of each book, we have included three words lists. Can your young learners find all the words in each book with the title letter in them?

Let's learn about the letter I.

3

The letter I can look like this: I.

The letter I can also look like this: i.

The letter **i** makes two different sounds.

One sound is the long sound,

like in the word island.

island

The other sound is the short sound,

like in the word inning.

inning

The letter **i** can be at the

beginning of a word, like igloo.

igloo

The letter **i** can be in the

middle of a word, like cabin.

cab**i**n

The letter **i** can be at the

end of a word, like macaroni.

macaron**i**

My name is **I**van. **I** like to imagine. **I** have

many dreams when **I** imagine. It is fun to

use my **i**magination.

I like to imagine places to visit.

I imagine an island in the Indian

Ocean. I like being alone on my

own tiny island.

I like to imagine an important baseball

 game. I imagine hitting the ball in the ninth

inning. It is the winning hit!

I like to imagine wintertime. **I** imagine

making a snow **i**gloo. It is an icy place

to play.

If **I** imagine springtime, **I** like to imagine

picking wildflowers. Or maybe **I** catch an

iguana instead!

It is exciting to imagine. **I** think of

many interesting things when **I**

imagine. What can you imagine?

Fun Facts

Igloo is the Inuit name for shelter. Inuit people are sometimes called Eskimos. **I**gloos can be made out of sod, wood, stone, or snow. The **i**gloo in this book is a snow **i**gloo. Snow igloos are made with blocks of ice. The blocks are fit together in a spiral that becomes smaller on top to form a dome. A hole in the top of the dome allows fresh air inside. The **i**gloo is the traditional house of the Inuit people, but almost no Inuit live in **i**gloos anymore.

Iguana is the name for certain large lizards. Most **i**guanas live in the Western Hemisphere. Unlike a lot of lizards, **i**guanas eat mostly plants. When there is very little food, an **i**guana can survive by using the fat stored in its neck and jaws. **I**guanas usually don't move very much. When attacked by predators, however, they use their tails like whips. And if a predator grabs the **i**guana's sharp tail, it will break off so the **i**guana can escape!

To Read More

About the Letter I

Ballard, Peg. *Little Bit: The Sound of Short I.* Chanhassen, Minn.: The Child's World, 2000.

Noyed, Robert. *Smiles: The Sound of Long I.* Chanhassen, Minn.: The Child's World, 2000.

About Igloos

Richter, Bernd C., and Susan E Richter. *Do Alaskans Live in Igloos? Show Me Your Alaska Home.* Cantwell, Alaska: Saddle Pal Creations, 1999.

Steltzer, Ulli. *Building an Igloo.* New York: Henry Holt, 1995.

About Iguanas

Johnston, Tony, and Mark Teague (illustrator). *The Iguana Brothers: A Tale of Two Lizards.* New York: Blue Sky Press, 1995.

Miller, Jake. *Green Iguana.* New York: PowerKids Press, 2003.

Words with I

**Words with I
at the Beginning**
I
icy
if
igloo
iguana
imagination
imagine
important
in
Indian
inning
instead
interesting
is
island
it
Ivan

**Words with I
in the Middle**
beginning
being
cabin
different
exciting
hit
hitting
imagination
imagine
Indian
inning
interesting
like
making
middle
ninth
picking
springtime
things
think
this
tiny
visit
wildflowers
winning
wintertime

**Words with I
at the End**
macaroni

About the Authors

Cynthia Klingel has worked as a high school English teacher and an elementary teacher. She is currently the curriculum director for a Minnesota school district. Cynthia Klingel lives with her family in Mankato, Minnesota.

Robert B. Noyed started his career as a newspaper reporter. Since then, he has worked in communications and public relations for a Minnesota school district for more than fourteen years. Robert B. Noyed lives with his family in Brooklyn Center, Minnesota.